RAFFKOR
THE STAMPEDING
BRUTE

With special thanks to Michael Ford
To Kenny Heffernan – Ireland's biggest
Beast Quest fan

www.beastquest.co.uk

ORCHARD BOOKS
338 Euston Road, London NW1 3BH
Orchard Books Australia
Level 17/207 Kent St, Sydney, NSW 2000

A Paperback Original
First published in Great Britain in 2014

Beast Quest is a registered trademark of Beast Quest Limited
Series created by Beast Quest Limited, London

Text © Beast Quest Limited 2014
Cover and inside illustrations by Steve Sims © Orchard Books 2014

A CIP catalogue record for this book is available from
the British Library.

ISBN 978 1 40832 920 7

3 5 7 9 10 8 6 4 2

Printed in Great Britain by CPI Group (UK) Ltd, Croydon, CR0 4YY

The paper and board used in this paperback are natural recyclable
products made from wood grown in sustainable forests. The
manufacturing processes conform to the environmental regulations of
the country of origin.

Orchard Books is a division of Hachette Children's Books,
an Hachette UK company

www.hachette.co.uk

Raffkor
THE STAMPEDING
BRUTE

Beast Quest®

THE CURSED DRAGON

BY ADAM BLADE

ORCHARD

Dear Reader

Do not pity me – my spells may be useless now, but my sixth sense will never go. Evil is afoot in this once peaceful kingdom. The Judge may have been defeated by brave Tom, but his minions do not rest. Our many Quests have taught me that an enemy beaten back will return stronger than before.

Tonight I had a vision of the pale moon turning black. What it means is not clear, but a new menace stalks the land of Rion, and I fear it will spread to Avantia. My wizard instincts tell me that our enemies plan to tip the balance of nature, turning good to evil. A hero will be needed to stand against the dark forces. Can you guess who that hero might be?

Aduro
Former Wizard to King Hugo

PROLOGUE

Wilfred the Beast Keeper panted hard as he took the final steps towards the caves. The climb from his hut down in the valley never got any easier. Still, the safety of the young Beasts was more important than a few aches in his legs.

The entrance to the caves was nearly invisible from the valley. Even the people of Rion had no idea what lived up here in the mountainside – young Beasts in training. Beasts which would one day protect innocent people in faraway kingdoms.

Entering the darkness of Raffkor's cave, Wilfred expected to find the young Bull Beast resting in his straw – but there was no sign of him.

"Odd…" muttered Wilfred, spying a trail of hoof-prints leading further into the depths of the cave. "Raffkor!" he called. "Come on, you lazy thing. We have training to be getting on with."

But there was no sound. Worry gnawed at Wilfred's mind. He hadn't brought a torch – normally, the pale blue glow that shone from Raffkor's horns would have provided him with enough light. The caves were pitch black today. He reached out blindly, using his hands to feel his way along the cold stone walls. He tripped, stumbling on the uneven ground.

There! A dim blue light seeped from

the gloom ahead. From out of the gloom came a snort, and then a series of panicked low grunts.

"Raffkor?" Wilfred called, as he rounded a corner.

Immediately, his feet skidded to a halt.

A tall woman stood in the centre of the cave, a cruel black whip raised above her head. Wilfred recognised her bright scarlet locks and the gold and silver symbols stitched into her flowing robe.

"Kensa!" he gasped.

"Nice of you to join us," said the sorceress.

Wilfred fumbled to draw his sword, but Kensa was too quick. With a flick of her wrist, a whip struck Wilfred's arm. He cried out in pain and the sword clattered to the ground. The sorceress lashed the whip across Raffkor's broad back. "Kill him!" she hissed.

The Beast moaned in pain and lowered his head to aim his four horns at Wilfred. Three of them glowed bright blue, while the fourth was blackened.

Wilfred dived aside as a bolt of blue light blasted from the Beast's horns. The Beast Keeper rolled across the rocky ground, scraping his knees and elbows, and his foot twisted painfully beneath him. When he looked up, he saw the bolt had torn a gash on the cave wall right where he'd been standing.

The Bull Beast stamped forward, snorting loudly.

"Raffkor, please!" said Wilfred. Trying to stand, he felt a flash of pain in his ankle. "Remember who I am!"

He saw no recognition in the bull's eyes, only hatred. He was under

Kensa's evil thrall. The blue energy
was swirling through Raffkor's horns,
building, building…

Wilfred cowered back against the cavern wall, which suddenly shook with a low rumble. Kensa's glance darted this way and that – she looked confused. With a crunch of breaking stone, the far side of the cave collapsed in on itself. A green, glittering shape surged into the space and daylight flooded the darkness.

"Vedra!" Wilfred mumbled.

The Green Dragon swept over Wilfred, snatching him up with his talons and carrying him away, up the mountainside.

"Don't let them escape!" Kensa screeched.

Vedra twisted in the sky, as a blue bolt shot from Raffkor's horns. Wilfred felt the air around him burn, as bright light forced his eyes closed. When he dared to open them again, the air was filled with smoke, and they were soaring above the mountain top. Raffkor and Kensa were lost beneath the clouds.

I'm alive, he thought with relief.

Vedra gave a keening cry as he lurched higher. Wilfred smelled burned flesh. With a sinking feeling, the Beast Keeper saw the deadly blast hadn't missed them completely. Across the dragon's green belly was a long, black scorch mark.

Vedra put his body in the way to save me, thought Wilfred. He looked down at the landscape flashing past. *What about the other young Beasts? Where are they?*

One thing was certain: Evil had come to Rion.

There was only one person who could help him now.

CHAPTER ONE

TOM'S REWARD

Storm lowered his head over the door of the stall as Tom fed him an apple.

"There you go, boy," he said. "You deserve more than just a treat and new shoes, but that will have to do for now."

"It's good to be together again, isn't it?" said Elenna. She was sitting on a hay bale, tightening her bowstring. Silver lounged on his belly beside her.

Tom nodded. He'd walked the Warrior's Road without his beloved steed, and had occasionally doubted they would ever be reunited. He'd only just triumphed on his last Quest.

A palace steward knocked at the stable door. "If you please, young sir and lady," he said, "His Majesty requests your presence in the Banqueting Hall."

"Of course!" said Elenna, leaping up. "I'd almost forgotten about dinner with King Hugo."

Tom ruffled Storm's mane and they followed the steward to the palace.

When the steward threw open the tall wooden doors, Tom gasped. He'd expected just King Hugo, the Wizard Daltec and Aduro, but the hall was packed with people. Courtiers, servants and soldiers filled the benches. Candles blazed in their holders and the tables groaned under the weight of platters of roasted meats, wheels of cheese and piles of fruit.

King Hugo stood up, raising a goblet. The room burst into wild applause. Flushing with embarrassment, Tom whispered, "Is this all for us?"

Elenna's eyes were wide. "It looks like it," she said.

"Let the festivities begin!" cried King Hugo, gesturing to the empty seats either side of him. Tom and Elenna made their way through the crowd, as people patted them on the back. Even Captain Harkman managed a smile, though it looked a little like a grimace.

"Good to have you home, Tom," he said.

Tom settled into the seat beside the King, and lowered his voice.

"Surely we're not celebrating *me*?" he asked. "The people of Avantia aren't supposed to know about the Beasts."

King Hugo grinned. "Of course not," he said. "Officially, we're here to celebrate the anniversary of my coronation."

Aduro smiled. "But unofficially, we'd like to thank you both for your courage in defending the kingdom."

The former Wizard rose from his seat and lifted his goblet. "A toast!" he declared. "To King Hugo's many years on the throne, and to many more!"

Tom and Elenna raised cups of fruit juice and joined in with the chorus.

"To King Hugo!"

Time seemed to fly past. Tom ate until

his stomach felt close to bursting.
Elenna passed scraps of meat beneath
the table to Silver. As the platters were
being cleared away, the music grew
louder, drowning out the voices of
the feasters. Tumblers and acrobats
began to perform in front of the weary
guests. King Hugo had already retired

to bed and Tom's eyelids were starting to droop as he watched a fire-breather. *I can't remember the last time I felt this tired*, he thought. Then he noticed that Daltec was beckoning him from the far side of the room. *What can he want?*

Tom nudged Elenna. "Something's wrong."

Silver yawned and got up, leaving the bone he'd been gnawing. Tom led the way towards the young Wizard.

"Is it the Judge?" Tom asked. Their enemy had vanished when they returned from the Warrior's Road, his evil plans defeated. "Has there been any news of him?"

"We've heard nothing," said Daltec, shaking his head. "The Circle of Wizards has banished him from their number. Aduro believes it will be some time before he regains enough strength to attack the kingdom again."

"Then what's wrong?" Elenna asked.

Daltec's face was grave. "Follow me."

He led them through a side door and along a narrow, unlit corridor. The air was cool after the crowded Banqueting Hall, and the sounds of the celebration grew muted.

They reached the end of the passage, and Daltec drew aside a heavy curtain. On the other side was a small chamber lit by a fire burning in the hearth. King Hugo sat in a chair in the centre of the room. *So he's not in bed, after all!* Aduro stood leaning on a staff at his side.

The King stood up. "I have a mission for you both," he said.

"A new Quest?" asked Tom, feeling a rush of anticipation. If a new threat had reached Avantia's shores, he was ready to face it.

"Something tells me that this Quest will be the hardest you have undertaken," Aduro added.

Tom sensed Elenna stiffen beside him. "Tell us," he said.

The King looked Tom straight in the eye. "You will go on an epic Quest..." His face split into a grin. "...to Errinel, where you will visit your aunt and uncle, and get some rest."

Tom frowned. "Rest?" he repeated. "What do you mean?"

The King placed both hands on Tom's shoulders. "You've defended Avantia from many enemies. It's time for you to stop looking for danger around every corner. You've earned a break."

"But..." Tom began. He caught a glimpse of Elenna grinning from the corner of his eye.

"That's an order," said King Hugo.

"You would not disobey your king, would you?"

Tom sighed. "No, Your Majesty," he said, and a fresh wave of weariness washed over him.

Perhaps a rest would be good, after all.

For the first time in ages, Tom would see his relatives again – and have nothing to do but eat cherry pie!

CHAPTER TWO

AN UNEXPECTED ARRIVAL

Tom woke feeling warm and snug on a feather-stuffed mattress. Morning light crept in between a crack in the shutters. Panic surged through his chest. He quickly threw off the blanket, looking for his sword and shield. Then he remembered: *I don't have to get up. There is no Quest…*

His beating heart slowing, he crossed

to the windows and opened the shutters. The sun was already above the castle walls. What time was it?

I haven't had a lie-in for so long, Tom thought. *Oh well, I'm following the King's orders.*

He dressed and headed down to the palace courtyard. Servants scurried about, preparing for the second day of the coronation celebrations. Some were hanging bunting over the main gate, others were carrying wood to make a bonfire. Tom found Elenna eating a plate of cheese outside the stables. She started laughing.

Tom frowned. "What's so funny?"

"Have you seen your hair?" she asked.

Tom walked over to a water trough and stared at his reflection. His thick brown hair was sticking up in all directions. Grinning, he scooped a handful of water over his head to smooth it down, then turned to his friend.

"Ready to go?" he asked. They'd planned the night before to head out together to Tom's village, Errinel. After that, Elenna would journey to the Western Shores to visit her fisherman uncle.

"Silver and I have been ready since dawn," she said, offering him the rest of her breakfast. "Here, you should eat before we set out."

Tom's stomach was rumbling, but he didn't want to delay any more. "I'm sure Aunt Maria will have baked," he said. "I can wait!"

After he'd saddled Storm, Elenna mounted behind him and they trotted out towards the gates.

Stands were being set up for a joust that would take place later that evening. As Storm clopped across the courtyard, Aduro shambled from the palace. He walked quickly, muttering to himself. Tom slowed his stallion and watched as the old Wizard made his way towards a low arched doorway.

The Secret Library, Tom thought. *I wonder why he's going in there.*

"Aduro!" Tom called.

His friend stopped in his tracks and spun round.

"Greetings," he said, quickly smiling. "I thought you would have left already."

The Wizard's smile didn't fool Tom. He could see the worry in Aduro's eyes.

"Is everything all right?" he asked.

"Oh, yes," said Aduro, throwing a glance at the library door. "Quite

all right. You two must be off. Enjoy
yourselves." Without waiting for a
reply, he ducked under the arch and
vanished down the library steps.

"He's acting oddly," Tom said to
Elenna. "Maybe we should follow
him?"

"You heard what he said," replied
Elenna. "There's nothing to worry

about. He's probably just researching some ancient spell books!"

Tom pushed his dark thoughts aside and gave Storm's flanks a nudge. "You're right. Let's get going – otherwise it'll be dark before we reach Errinel."

"And more importantly," said Elenna, "your uncle might have eaten all the cherry pie!"

Captain Harkman stood over the gate-tower, and gave Tom a wave.

"It's all right for some," he called down. "I don't get a day off!" He pointed to a soldier manning the battlements. "Nor do you. Stop slouching!"

Both Tom and Elenna laughed as Storm crossed the drawbridge out into the fields beyond.

The sun had risen to its peak, warming Tom's back as they galloped down the dusty road that led out of the City. Silver kept pace beside them, his tongue lolling. Other travellers on the road waved and watched them fly past. The crops in the fields were almost ready to harvest. Golden ears of corn fluttered in the light breeze. Tom's heart surged to see the kingdom at peace after so many Quests. With their enemies defeated and evil at bay, balance had returned to Avantia.

A sudden shadow fell over them. Tom glanced up, and his breath caught in his throat as he reined Storm to a halt. Something dark was passing behind the pale clouds ahead – something quick and huge. Silver was growling, pawing at the earth.

"What in all Avantia?" muttered Elenna.

Storm tossed his head, nostrils flaring. Tom smelled it too – sulphur.

"A dragon!" he said, sliding from Storm's back and drawing his sword. *A new enemy…*

But as a green, scaled body broke through the clouds, Tom realised this was no foe, but a friend. "It's Vedra!"

The dragon had grown even more since Tom last saw him in Rion. He was almost the size of Ferno now. His mighty wings heaved up and down, but not fast enough to stop him falling. Something was wrong.

Tom watched as the dragon slid out of the sky, straining to keep his head aloft. Across his belly was a black scar, like a burn. A figure crouched low against his back.

"He's going to crash!" said Elenna.

With a moan, Vedra slammed into the ground, throwing up clods of soil and making the earth rumble. The figure on Vedra's back somersaulted across the field, sprawling into the long grass with a cry. Tom recognised him at once.

"That's Wilfred!" he exclaimed. "The Beast Keeper of Rion."

CHAPTER THREE

THE WOUNDED DRAGON

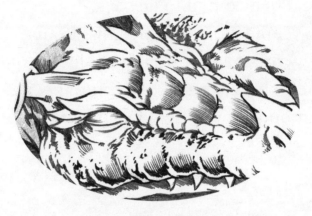

Tom rushed to Wilfred's side. The Beast Keeper was sitting up, rubbing his head. His face was gaunt, his hair windswept. Tom saw blisters on his hands and realised he must have been gripping Vedra's scales for dear life on the perilous flight from Rion.

"Great danger…" mumbled Wilfred. "Beasts cursed… Evil…"

"Quiet for now," said Elenna, arriving at Tom's side. "Just be still, Wilfred."

She cushioned his head in her hands and helped him to lie back.

Vedra let out a pained hiss from a few paces away. He tried to lift his neck, but it sagged back onto the ground. One wing flapped weakly, the

other was folded beneath his body. It might have been broken.

Tom looked desperately around. He had to get the dragon to safety, but the crash would have been heard for miles. He could not let the people of Avantia know about the existence of the Beasts.

"Other travellers will pass this way," he said. "We need to hide Vedra."

Elenna looked aghast. "But how? We can't possibly move a dragon!"

The air sizzled and in a puff of smoke, Daltec appeared beside them. Silver jumped back in surprise.

"I saw what happened in my crystal ball," said the young Wizard.

"Can you magic Vedra back to the palace?" asked Tom.

Daltec shook his head. "Even when Aduro still had his magic, he would have struggled to move such a big Beast," he said. "The King is sending a platoon of his strongest troops, with horses to draw Vedra to the palace."

Muttering a spell, he pointed at the dragon. Blue light swirled from his fingertips, wrapping itself around Vedra's body. When the light cleared, an enormous cart had appeared beneath the Good Beast.

Vedra's flanks rose and fell quickly, as if he was struggling to breathe. Daltec frowned. "Now let me think...how does it go?" He pointed again.

*"Clouds and cloaks, shadows and lies,
Hide this creature from human eyes."*

A velvet blanket appeared in the air and draped itself over the Beast. Soon, the cart and the dragon had vanished.

"We need to be quick," said Daltec. "The concealment spell won't last for long." He crouched beside Wilfred, placing a hand on the Beast Keeper's head and muttering another spell.

With a gasp, Wilfred opened his eyes and struggled into a sitting position. He stared straight at Tom. "Terrible Evil," he said. "I had to come and warn you. Avantia is in danger!"

Night had fallen over the City, and all the celebrations had been cancelled. The guests had been told that King Hugo was ill, but the truth was far worse. The King sat with his head resting on his hands in the cellar beneath the palace. Vedra lay curled in the centre of the room, sleeping fitfully. Despite the late hour and the long march back to the palace with the hidden cart, Tom was wide awake.

Daltec and Aduro had been talking to
Wilfred for some time, looking closely
at the black burn on Vedra's belly.

Is it my imagination, Tom wondered,
or is the wound growing?

"Well, Daltec?" asked the King.

"Your Majesty, it's not good."

Tom swallowed. "Will Vedra die?"

"Worse," said Daltec. "The Green Dragon has been poisoned with Lunar Blood. Evil is spreading through his veins as we speak. By the next Full Moon, the transformation will be complete – Vedra's scales will turn black and he will no longer be a Good Beast."

Aduro looked cross with himself. "I sensed trouble brewing," he mumbled. "That's why I was in the library poring over ancient scrolls. I should have acted…"

Tom's fists clenched at his sides. "There must be something we can do to save him." He remembered the day the twin dragons had hatched – how he'd kept them safe from harm. *There's no way I'm giving up on Vedra now!*

Aduro clutched a sheaf of old

parchment. "There is one cure...but it means completing a dangerous Quest."

Tom gripped his sword hilt. "Then we'll leave at once."

Aduro held up his hand. "The old books say there's only one remedy for the evil that infects Vedra – the Gilded Elixir. Its four ingredients are found in the four corners of the kingdom. You must travel far, and quickly, if you're to gather them in time."

"Storm is already saddled," said Tom, walking towards the door. "Do you have a map for me?"

Aduro nodded, and held up the parchment in his hand. "It's not as simple as finding the ingredients," said the former Wizard. "Kensa will certainly have laid traps in your way."

"Kensa the Witch!" said Tom. "So she's behind this?"

"That's right," said Aduro. "With the Judge gone, I knew it would not be long before she started causing her own trouble, but I didn't think she would act so quickly." He lowered his head towards King Hugo. "I should have warned you sooner, Your Majesty."

"We must all be wary," said the King. "Evil never rests."

Wilfred was wringing his hands. "I tried to stop her," he said, "but she had already turned Raffkor to Evil. Vedra was wounded trying to save me."

Elenna rested a comforting hand on the Beast Keeper's shoulder. "You couldn't have known Kensa's plans. Don't worry, we will stop her."

Tom looked at his friend. "That's right. But time is precious – and we've wasted enough already. Let's go!"

CHAPTER FOUR

A NEW QUEST

Aduro spread out an old map on
a table. "I found this in the library
as well, tucked into the back of an
ancient book." He pointed to the four
corners in turn. "Your first destination
is the Northern Mountains. From
there you'll head south to the Ruby
Desert, then east to the Dark Jungle.
The last journey will be north again –
to the Pit of Fire."

Tom added up the vast distances in his head. *We won't have time to cover that much ground before the next Full Moon…*

From Elenna's creased forehead, he guessed she was thinking the same thing.

"You haven't told him about the others?" said Wilfred from the corner of the room.

"Others?" said Elenna.

Daltec shared a glance with Aduro. "The other Beasts of Rion," said the young Wizard. "We don't know what has happened to them. My crystal ball is blank. It's likely they too are under Kensa's spells."

"Raffkor didn't seem to recognise me at all," said Wilfred. "He attacked me!"

Tom recalled the brave young

Bull-Beast from his last visit to Rion. Then Raffkor had been stubborn, but good at heart. *If he's turned Evil, this Quest just got even harder.* "What about Falra?" Tom asked. "And Vislak? And Tikron? Surely they can't all be cursed?"

"I'm afraid it looks that way," said Aduro. "Kensa will use every weapon she has against you. You will be fighting Beasts who were once your allies."

Tom felt his hopes fading, but he tapped his shield. "At least I can summon the Good Beasts to help me."

Aduro shook his head. "If Kensa has magic to corrupt Good Beasts, it's too risky – she might be able to turn more of them to Evil. It would stack the odds even higher against you. No, I'm afraid you two must tackle this Quest alone."

"Not alone," said Wilfred. He dried his eyes. "I'm coming too. It's my duty to protect these Beasts."

Tom looked at the young man doubtfully. "Kensa and Sanpao will have no mercy," he said. "You'll be safer here."

Wilfred's face fell.

"You will not be facing Sanpao this time," said Daltec.

"What do you mean?" asked Elenna. "Wherever Kensa goes, the Pirate King is never far behind."

"Since you left to walk the Warrior's Road, he and Kensa have fallen out," said Daltec. "The sorceress is now working alone."

Tom folded the map and tucked it into his tunic. Daltec held out a leather sack, studded with iron and stitched with silver thread.

"Place the ingredients in this," he said. "The first one you will need to find is Starleaf. It grows only on the

Murmuring Peak – one of the tallest of the Northern Mountains."

As he and Elenna rushed to the stables, Tom felt like a fool. *To think I was going to go to Errinel and rest. I should have realised something was wrong.*

Storm whinnied impatiently. *He senses the danger too*, thought Tom.

As Tom swung himself into the saddle, Wilfred came running into the courtyard after him. He wore a travelling cloak. "Don't try to talk me out of it," he said. "I'm coming with you."

Perhaps I was wrong about the Beast Keeper, thought Tom. He sensed a steely fighting spirit beneath Wilfred's pale skin. After all, hadn't the young man ridden a dragon all the way to Avantia from Rion?

"You'll find Breeze in there," Tom said, nodding towards the stables. "Saddle her up. We ride at once!"

CHAPTER FIVE

RETURN TO THE NORTH

The long gallop had left Storm's neck slick with sweat. Now, Tom rode half asleep, lulled by the rhythmic drumming of the horse's cantering hooves. He felt Elenna's grip on his waist tighten.

"We're almost there," she muttered.

Tom looked up to see the glorious peaks of the Northern Mountains

silhouetted against the dawn light. His
fingers were cramping on the reins.
They had ridden for two nights, only
stopping so the horses could drink from
streams. Even Silver looked weary after
the long slog across fields and farms and
open plains. Each time Tom had been
tempted to stop, he imagined Kensa's
grinning face and it drove him on. *How
could she poison the hearts of innocent young
Beasts?* The depths of her cruelty knew
no bounds.

Colour seeped into the mountains as
the sun rose higher. Tom felt a shudder
of recognition. One of his first Quests
had brought him here – to free Arcta
the Mountain Giant from Malvel's Evil
enchantment.

Tom urged Storm up the narrow,
dusty paths. The horse's hooves
skittered, but Storm was used to placing

his feet carefully. Wilfred came behind on Breeze. The Beast Keeper clutched the horse's neck in panic – he was not a natural rider.

"Keep an eye out for Kensa," Tom told them.

The first village they came to made Tom's blood run cold. The simple stone buildings lay in ruins, crushed under boulders that had tumbled from above. There were no people in sight.

"Has there been an earthquake?" asked Elenna.

"Only a Beast could cause such a powerful tremor," said Tom.

"Raffkor," whispered Wilfred. Tom saw the Beast Keeper's skin was pale. "He used to love causing landslides when he was untrained and mischievous. I managed to channel his anger, but Kensa must be using it for Evil."

The next settlement was the same,
and so was the next – just deserted,
collapsed homes, half buried under
rubble. Tom saw a child's wooden
soldier puppet lying broken on the
ground. His heart hardened. *I can't let
these people down*, he thought.

As they picked their way through the debris, a distant tremor shook the ground, and more stones rattled down. "We're getting closer," said Tom. He wasn't sure how he felt about facing Raffkor. *Can I find it in my heart to fight a friend?*

Human voices interrupted his thoughts.

"Quiet!" he warned his companions.

Tom quickly slid off Storm's back and ran in a crouch to a low rise ahead. He peered over the top as Elenna and Wilfred joined him.

A group of men and women were carrying makeshift picks, axes and staffs as they climbed the mountain slope. The ground was rough, with shallow ravines filled with strewn boulders. The group had a pack of dogs with them, straining at their leashes. Some of their clothes were torn and dirty. *They must be from the abandoned villages*, Tom thought.

"Are you sure it's this way, Ched?" asked a woman.

The bearded man who was leading the group shot her an angry look. "The dogs can smell something," he said. "When we find what's causing the rockfalls, we can kill it – then our misery will be over."

"But how can you be sure there's something up there?" asked the woman.

Ched stared up the mountain. "There's nothing natural about these landslides," he said. "They happen when the weather is calm. And you've heard the strange bellowing – and the roars."

At that very moment, the ruby

in Tom's belt began to glow, and a message crept into his head. *People come. People angry.*

Tom recognised the voice as Arcta's.

Wilfred made to stand, but Tom pulled him back.

"Wait!" he said.

"But they'll kill Raffkor," said the Beast Keeper, "...or he'll kill them!"

"No, they won't," said Tom, pulling out his map. "If I'm right, it's another scent those dogs are following." He showed the map to Elenna, and pointed at a spot between two looming peaks. "Do you remember this place?"

Elenna's eyes widened. "Arcta's lair!"

Tom nodded grimly. "Arcta's a friendly Beast, but if these mountain folk attack him, he'll defend himself. We have to stop them, but there are only three of us. We have to be clever."

People close, came Arcta's voice.

Tom scanned the horizon and –
There! – the Mountain Giant's shaggy head was peering above a ridge. The villagers were heading right for him!

Tom touched the red jewel and sent

a warning to his friend: *Stay out of sight.*

Arcta dipped behind the ridge again, but Tom could sense his fear and confusion. He needed a better plan. He had to keep Arcta calm and stop the villagers before they reached the Beast's lair.

"I've got it," he said, slipping his shield off his shoulder. "Wilfred, take this." He removed the feather from his shield – the token he'd won from Arcta when they first faced one another. He handed it to the Beast Keeper.

Wilfred frowned. "What am I supposed to do with this?"

Tom traced a loop on the map. "Ride ahead, around the search party. Go to Arcta." Wilfred went white. "Don't worry," said Tom. "This feather will tell him you can be trusted. He'll realise I must have given it to you. I want you to try and keep him from breaking cover. Reassure him."

"What if he doesn't understand me?" said Wilfred.

Tom frowned. "Hopefully the feather will be enough. You must have gestures you use when training Beasts."

"They work on young Beasts, yes," said Wilfred. "Arcta's fully grown!"

"You can do it," said Elenna. "We believe in you."

Wilfred took the feather, and climbed back onto Breeze. "I won't let you down."

He set off at a canter and soon disappeared over a rocky shelf, staying out of sight of the search party along a sunken path.

"And what are you going to do?" asked Elenna.

"Cause a distraction," Tom replied. "Can you stay here and guard the animals in case anyone comes?"

Elenna nodded. "Good luck."

Tom set off at a run, darting low between boulders to avoid being spotted. Luckily the search party were all looking ahead of themselves, so Tom headed up the slope at their backs. He was breathing hard by the time he reached the top, which was scattered with more rocks. The hunters had almost reached the spot where Arcta was hiding. There wasn't much time. *I hope Wilfred can convince Arcta to stay put!*

CHAPTER SIX

A VILLAGE IN FEAR

Tom drew his sword, and buried its point beneath a boulder the size of a barrel. He heaved, trying to lever the boulder down the slope. It didn't budge. *I have to try harder.*

Summoning the power of his golden breastplate, he pushed again. Magical strength flowed through his arms and the boulder tipped, beginning to roll down the slope. As it bounced along, it smashed more rocks, creating a hail of earth and stone.

Tom saw the party of villagers stop and look back. The rockfall had missed them by a hundred paces, just as Tom had planned. He waited, hoping they would turn back to investigate the landslide. The dogs were still nosing the other way – towards Arcta.

Tom held his breath.

"The creature must have circled behind us," the leader called, pointing towards the settling dust. He began hurrying towards it, his companions following.

Tom let out a sigh of relief, and hurried back to Elenna.

"You did it!" she said with a grin.

But Tom couldn't bring himself

to smile. "We've lost precious time already," he said, pointing along a path that led eastwards towards a sharp peak. "The map says the Starleaf is that way."

Ched and the villagers had disappeared over the ridge of the mountain, so Tom and Elenna set off with the animals, back along the path.

Soon they reached another settlement, directly on their route. Tom's spirits lifted a little when he saw it was intact. Smoke rose from chimneys and people milled around the houses and market stalls.

"At least Raffkor's havoc hasn't reached this far," he said to Elenna.

As Tom climbed off Storm to lead him through the market, Silver growled in warning.

Tom spun around, and saw the
villagers had all stopped dead,
watching Tom and Elenna with cold
eyes.

"We don't welcome looters here,"
said a young woman.

More of the crowd edged closer.
Some were snatching up weapons.

"We've had enough of your sort,"
said a grizzled man with muscular
arms. "Just because your village has
been destroyed, don't think that
you're welcome in ours."

"Tom!" hissed Elenna.

He turned and saw the search
party from the mountain, their faces

twisted with hate. The dogs were drooling, baring their teeth. *This must be their village!*

"What have we got here?" said the leader, Ched, in a low, menacing voice. He didn't look happy to see them.

Tom resisted the urge to reach for his sword. "We're not looters!" he said, as Silver snapped his head back and forth.

"The boy's got a blade, Ched," said the woman. "And the girl's got a bow."

The bearded man stepped forward. "Why do you carry weapons?"

"We..." Tom couldn't think of anything to say. He couldn't tell them the truth, about the Beasts and their Quest. "We're here on the King's business," he said at last.

The villager narrowed his eyes. "And what business is that?"

Tom could feel the suspicion growing from every side. "King Hugo has asked us…" He paused, searching for a reason. "He has asked us…"

The crowd pressed closer.

"We're here to investigate the rockfalls," said Elenna. "The King takes his subjects' plight very seriously."

There were mutterings of approval from the villagers. "About time the King sent someone," said Selima.

"We've seen the other villages affected," added Tom. "It's terrible to behold."

Many lowered their weapons, including Ched.

"Then you're welcome here," he said. "Ask whatever you require, and we will do our best to help you. We've heard strange sounds echoing in the mountains – like an animal in a rage."

Tom kept his features calm. The last thing he wanted was for the villagers to know what was actually making the noises.

"The wind makes odd sounds sometimes," he said.

Ched shrugged. "Not like this. We fear our village will be next," he said.

Tom clapped him on the arm. "Don't worry," he said. "We're here now."

"Before you continue," said the leader, "you must have a nice cool drink to prepare you for your climb. Follow me."

Tom felt a twinge of frustration. Every moment was precious on this

Quest to find the Starleaf.

"Be patient," said Elenna, obviously sensing his thoughts. "We mustn't blow our cover."

Ched led them through the market, to a stall with a painted sign showing oranges.

"Freshly squeezed juice," rasped a woman in a thick hooded shawl and long cloak. Tom couldn't see her face but she sounded elderly.

He wasn't thirsty, but Elenna was right – they had an act to keep up.

"Two cups, please," he said, moving closer. Storm strained against the reins slightly. "We'll be on our way soon," he told his horse.

The old woman dropped an armful of oranges into a strange device shaped like a cylinder. She turned a handle and juice dribbled from

a spout into a waiting cup. "You'll
never forget Asnek's juice," she said,
still winding the handle.

Silver paced back and forth. *He
doesn't like all these people around him,*
thought Tom.

The cloaked stallholder filled one
cup and placed another under the
spout. She handed Tom and Elenna a

cup each. Tom noticed that her hands were unwrinkled. *Perhaps she isn't as old as she sounds.*

"How much do we owe you?" Elenna asked.

The woman waved dismissively. "For two servants of the King? Nothing! It's my pleasure!"

"Thank you," said Tom.

Silver leaped up, placing his front paws on the table and sending oranges scattering onto the floor.

"Silver, no!" said Elenna, pushing him back and apologising to the stallholder. "I don't know what's got into him."

"No matter," said the woman. "Tell me, do you expect to return from your investigation in the mountains?"

What a strange question, Tom thought. "I hope so. Here's to a

successful mission," he said, raising
his cup of delicious-smelling juice.

Elenna touched her cup to his.
As she went to take a drink, Silver
jumped up again and nipped her arm.

"Ouch!" she said. The cup fell from
her hand. "Silver, whatever is the
matt—"

Smoke rose up from the ground,
making a hissing noise as the rock at

Elenna's feet melted where the juice
had spilled.

"Acid!" Tom gasped.

CHAPTER SEVEN

FIGHTING AN OLD ENEMY

Tom threw his cup aside, drawing his sword and pointing the tip of the blade at the cloaked figure.

"Who are you?" he demanded.

The woman straightened up, rising a head taller than Tom, and pulled back her hood, revealing bright red hair and a cruel, narrow face. The figure threw off her cloak to show a black velvet robe marked with strange symbols and lightning bolts. Her walking stick magically grew into a carved silver staff.

The villagers gasped and drew back.

"How nice to see you again," said Kensa. "Now prepare to die!"

With a flick of her staff, the table tipped and the cup of acid flew towards Tom's head. He ducked and the liquid shot past his face, hissing as it splashed the ground behind him. Tom turned to make sure no one else was hurt, then felt Kensa's foot catch him in the stomach and send him sprawling across the ground. His sword flew from his grasp, and his head slammed against a rock.

Through blurred vision, Tom saw Kensa stoop to snatch up his sword, then pounce forward, slicing it at

him. Tom rolled, hearing the steel bite into rock and villagers cry out as they scattered to safety.

Tom sprang to his feet as Kensa rushed at him, her staff and Tom's sword cutting rapid arcs. Tom used both hands to grip his shield as the blows slammed into him. He'd fought many skilled warriors in his time, but facing Kensa was like tackling three fighters at once. Silver growled and paced closer, but Tom's flashing blade drove him back to Elenna's side. As Tom spun to avoid being cut in two by the sword, he caught a glimpse of Elenna. She had an arrow to her bowstring. "I can't get a clear shot!" she cried.

Tom knew that he and Kensa were moving around too quickly for Elenna to dare fire an arrow. If she missed Kensa, she'd hit an innocent villager.

"Throw me your bow!" Tom cried.

Elenna tossed it to him. Kensa jabbed with Tom's sword, and he sidestepped to catch the bow. He felt the power of the amber jewel in his belt, making him move lightning-fast to slip the bow under Kensa's guard and jab her hard in the ribs. The Witch doubled up, gasping for breath. Tom swung his weapon and smashed it into Kensa's legs, knocking her feet from beneath her. Kensa landed on her back with a cry. Leaping forward, Tom stepped on her wrist, pinning her sword-arm to the ground. Silver pounced onto her other arm, so she couldn't use her staff either.

"It's over," said Tom, pressing the bow-tip against the Witch's throat. She squirmed, then fell back with a grimace.

"All right," she said weakly. "You win."

Tom handed the bow back to

Elenna and bent over to claim his sword.

Oof!

Kensa twisted free and kicked Tom in the thigh. He fell to one knee as pain shot up his leg. Kensa's other foot caught Silver in the middle, and the wolf rolled over, yelping. In the blink of an eye, Kensa was on her feet and sprinting through the crowd, swiping with her staff to keep the villagers at bay.

"Out of the way, cretins!" she cried.

Elenna helped Tom to his feet. "Are you badly hurt?"

Tom shook his head. "I'll be fine. We've wasted enough time here. Let's find the Starleaf."

The murmuring voices around them fell silent. Tom looked up and saw hostile faces watching him.

Ched pushed his way to the front of the group, his eyes as hard as flint. "Starleaf? I thought you were here to look into the rockfalls?"

Tom glanced to Elenna – but this time she gave a helpless shrug.

"It's complicated," Tom said. "We think the Starleaf and the rockfalls are connected."

Ched snatched up a hammer from the blacksmith's stall, and brandished it at Tom.

"We know they're connected. The Starleaf growing up there on the Murmuring Peak…" He motioned to the mountain above the village. "It's the only thing keeping us safe. That rare plant has long been lucky to our people."

"You lied to us," said Selima. She had an axe in her hands.

"You will not get anywhere near our Starleaf," said Ched.

Tom took a deep breath and stepped forward. "We may not have told you the full truth," he said loudly and clearly, "but we are still servants of

King Hugo. Please, trust us."

He hoped the villagers would back down. Some of them were looking at the ground, unsure of themselves, but Ched only sneered.

"We trust nobody. You're a long way from the palace, young ones. No one in King Hugo's city can hear you scream."

As the villagers' faces turned ugly, Tom knew Ched was right.

CHAPTER EIGHT

THE MURMURING PEAK

The crowd closed in, weapons clutched in their fists.

We must be outnumbered twenty to one, thought Tom. There was only one way out. He glanced at Elenna, and knew she was thinking the same thing as him.

"Now!" he cried, leaping for Storm's reins and swinging himself into the saddle. Elenna vaulted up behind him. With a kick, Tom sent the stallion charging straight at Ched. The village leader jumped aside, not even trying to swing his hammer. Looking over his shoulder, Tom saw Silver scampering through the gap they'd created.

"Seize them!" bellowed Ched.

Storm leaped over a market cart

and thundered across the square. A few villagers tried to grab his reins, but he was too quick and powerful to be stopped. Stones whizzed past Tom's ears, but soon Storm was carrying them away from the village along a mountain track.

"Something tells me they don't like strangers," said Elenna, when they were at a safe distance.

"Kensa's probably poisoned their thoughts against us," said Tom. "Who knows how long she was waiting for us there?"

They lurched as Storm stumbled to a stop, giving a pained whinny. Tom looked down and saw blood oozing from a gash at the top of his leg.

"A stone must have hit him," said Tom, climbing down.

Elenna dismounted too. "It doesn't

look too bad," she said, inspecting the wound. "I have some herbs that will help."

Tom took out his map. By his reckoning, the mountain called the Murmuring Peak was the one that rose steeply above them right now. Somewhere, up there, was a Beast under Kensa's thrall. "Then I'll make the climb alone," he said.

"Are you sure?" said Elenna.

Tom nodded. "You stay here and look after Storm." He paused. "And if I don't make it back, continue the Quest without me."

Elenna's expression was grave. "You'll make it," she said.

Tom smiled, and set off up the mountainside.

At first the going was hard, but not treacherous. Raffkor's tremors had loosened the rocks, so each time Tom put his foot higher it slid backwards a little. But then it became steeper. Tom rested his hands on the slope and looked upwards into a gusting wind that blew dust into his eyes. He thought he made out a safe route, where the rock looked firmest, and reached up with his hands. He heaved himself upwards, feeling the burn in his shoulders. Anchoring his feet, he searched for the next handhold. *If I fall, at least I'll be protected by Arcta's eagle feath—*

CRACK!

The rock crumbled away. Panic surged through Tom's stomach as he clung by his fingertips to the cliff face.

Oh no! I gave the feather to Wilfred!

A sickly feeling of dread came over Tom as he looked down. If he lost his

grip now, he was dead.

I can't turn back…Vedra is relying on me.

He was panting as he found safe points for his toes in a narrow crack. The gusts whistled off the peak like whispering voices. *No wonder they call it the Murmuring Peak*, he thought.

Pressing on, he chose his path with extra care. The wind teased at his clothes, threatening to pull him to his death. *Turn back*, the mountain seemed to whisper. *This is one fight too far, even for you.*

Tom shook his head to clear the voices. *It's just my imagination.* He was glad to reach a narrow ledge where he could rest. Breathing hard, he looked back and spied Elenna, just a small dot far below.

You'll never succeed, boomed a voice.

Tom almost lost his footing. "That was no wind!" he muttered.

Vedra will fall into my mistress's power. Then all your Good Beasts will follow.

Tom realised the voice was coming through the ruby in his belt.

"Raffkor," he muttered.

Give up, said the voice in his head.

You're no match for me.

Tom reached for the next handhold. "I'm a match for any Beast!"

A crunching sound made him glance up. The rock shook under his fingertips and deadly chips of stone rained down. Tom pressed himself against the rock face and felt the rush of debris fall past. *So Raffkor's waiting for me up there. If I even make it, that is.*

He continued to climb, trying to ignore the thought of what awaited him. Raffkor stamped again further up the mountain, and more stone cascaded down.

You could only just handle me back in Rion, said Raffkor's voice. *I'm ten times stronger now.*

Tom recalled training with Raffkor under Wilfred's watchful eye on a previous Quest. It was true that the

Bull Beast had been a fearsome creature. *We were just playing then*, he said in his mind, sending his thoughts to the Beast. *This time, we fight for real.*

Tom peered up. Ten arm-lengths separated him from the next ledge. And standing on the ledge above that was the muscular blue body of Raffkor. Three of his horns shone with blue light, the source of his power. The fourth was blackened, just as Vedra's belly had been. He, too, had been poisoned with Lunar Blood.

The Bull Beast snorted, and swung his massive head.

I'm waiting for you, Tom, he said.

CHAPTER NINE

BATTLE ON THE LEDGE

Tom heaved himself onto the first ledge. His arms were trembling from the climb, but he tried not to let the pain show in his face.

Raffkor raked one hoof along the ground above Tom, his flanks rising and falling with rapid breaths. Tom felt his stomach twist in fear. Raffkor was at least twice as large as when they'd last met. The bull's face wore a wild, mad stare, his nostrils flaring as drool spilled from his black lips. Back in Rion, Raffkor had been unruly, but good-natured. Now his snorting breath and heaving flanks seemed full of hate.

The Beast lowered his head, aiming his horns. One of them was jet black.

Perhaps that's the answer, Tom thought, remembering Vedra's black burn. *If I can slice off the blackened horn, maybe that will free Raffkor from Kensa's Evil enchantment.*

With a furious snort, Raffkor leaped down from his ledge. He landed with a bone-shuddering crunch. Tom lowered his shield to his arm and drew his sword. Raffkor towered over him. The blue swirls of light that sheathed his horns glowed brighter.

"I know your heart is good," Tom said.

The Bull Beast tossed his head angrily and stalked forward.

"Remember when we fought side by side, in Rion?" Tom called, trying to remind the Beast.

Raffkor bellowed, shaking his tail like a whip.

"Kensa is not your friend," Tom said. "She's Evil!"

Raffkor let out a snort of fury and charged, covering the ground between them in a flash. Tom scrambled away, using the power of the amber jewel to guide his sword in a defensive slash. The Beast's hot breath blasted his face. Raffkor stopped, then lunged once more.

Tom's foot slipped away from beneath him, and he threw himself against the cliff face, wheeling for balance. His skin went cold as he peered over the abyss. *I almost fell...*

The ledge was only just wide

enough for Tom. Raffkor dared not come any closer. Instead he took two steps back, and stamped his hooves angrily. Tom clung to the rocks.

"While there's blood in my veins," he said, "you'll have to do better than that!"

Raffkor lowered his head. His horns flared and Tom raised his shield just in time. A bolt of blue fire shot from the Beast's head and sizzled over the wooden surface. Tom's shield grew so hot that it burned his skin. Blisters started to bulge and the pain was too much to bear. He flung the shield away, watching with horror as his only protection spiralled into the nothingness below. He drew his sword, but he was too far from the Beast to use it.

Prepare to die, boomed Raffkor's

voice in Tom's head.

He fired another blast. This time Tom slashed with his sword. The blade deflected the blue bolt and sent it sizzling back towards the Beast. Raffkor scampered aside in panic as the fire cut a gash in the cliff wall.

The Bull Beast's glowing eyes watched Tom intently. *He doesn't dare use his magic again*, thought Tom, *in case it deflects back and strikes him. But there's no way I can get close to him either. It's a stalemate. Unless…*

Tom called out to the Bull Beast, goading him: "Kensa should never have chosen such a weak Beast to defend the Starleaf." He faked a mocking laugh. "Fighting you is a waste of my time."

The blue glow was building in the Beast's horns. *He's getting ready to unleash a huge bolt*, thought Tom. *Just what I need.*

Raffkor roared and fired a blinding flash of blue light. Tom swung his sword to meet it. His arms shook as his blade sent the power scorching back at the Beast.

Blue rays exploded from Raffkor's head as the bolt slammed right between his eyes. He rocked back on his legs, then toppled sideways with a crash.

This is my chance! Tom squinted through the flash and leaped forward. Raffkor wouldn't be stunned for long. The Beast began to find its feet again, bellowing in fury and pain, but Tom was bringing his blade down at the base of the blackened horn.

Shockwaves shot up Tom's arm as the steel lodged halfway through the horn. Black gore spurted from the cut. Raffkor tossed his massive head and Tom heaved his sword free. The Beast batted at the rocks with his hooves. Tom stepped back, gripped the hilt in both hands and swung again. This time the blade sheared clean through the horn.

Raffkor's roars shook the mountainside. As the black horn fell down into the abyss below, the Beast tossed his head.

Tom scrambled back to avoid being smashed in the chest. *It hasn't worked!*

Raffkor's mouth frothed with spit. Tom didn't know what to do. He couldn't kill a Good Beast, but he had to defend himself.

Raffkor's eyes rolled back madly, showing just the whites. Then he charged.

Tom had no choice. He raised his sword, aiming it at the Beast's heart.

CHAPTER TEN

FINDING THE STARLEAF

Raffkor skidded to a halt, close enough that Tom could smell the lingering stench of Evil. The Beast's sides rose in a deep breath, but his eyes were still and calm. His nostrils no longer blasted gouts of steam. The Beast's legs trembled as the sweat dried in his matted fur.

Through the ruby in his belt, Tom

heard a voice filled with shame.

I am sorry, Master of the Beasts.

Tom's racing pulse began to beat more slowly. Now he sensed only goodness in the Beast before him. Slowly, he lowered his sword, then slid it into his sheath. He held out a hand and touched Raffkor's head where the black horn had been.

"There's nothing to be sorry for," he said. "You were under Kensa's Evil enchantment."

You saved me, came back Raffkor's message. *You took away the Evil in my body.* So Tom's actions had worked, after all! Slicing off the black horn had been the right thing to do – but only just in time. A moment later, and Tom would have been lying in a pool of his own blood now.

He felt a wave of anger from the

Beast, as if Raffkor was remembering his encounter with the cruel sorceress.

Tom focused, willing a message to the Beast. *If you really want to get your own back on Kensa, help me find the Starleaf.*

Raffkor sank to the ground, lying flat. *Climb on*, he said.

Tom gripped the tuft of hair at the base of Raffkor's neck, and hauled himself onto the broad back. The huge body rocked beneath him as the Beast lumbered to a standing position, his flank muscles rippling. With a lurch, Raffkor leaped to the ledge above, hooves crushing stone. Then he began to run, sure-footed, along the narrow ridge. Tom tried not to look down. This was so different from sitting in Storm's saddle. Each

bone-crunching step almost shook
him loose.

Soon they reached a plateau right
on the top of the Murmuring Peak
and Raffkor paused. Tom looked
around. Clouds whipped past, giving

everything a ghostly appearance.

A voice drifted up from far below. Not the winds this time, but Elenna.

"Tom? Are you all right?"

Tom cupped his hands to his mouth. "I'm fine!" he called. "And so is Raffkor! We're going to find the Starleaf."

As the clouds cleared, Tom gazed in every direction at the mountains spread out around them. *Avantia looks so peaceful from up here – though nothing could be further from the truth.*

Among the barren rocks, his eyes fell on a few green sprigs. "The Starleaf!" he cried, sliding off Raffkor's back.

Tom approached one of the plants. Its broad, stiff leaves were shaped into five points and covered in a fine fur. A fierce wind ripped across the mountain top, chilling Tom's skin. As he turned his head from the gale, his breath caught in his throat.

"Your horn!" he said. "It's grown back!"

Raffkor, untroubled by the freezing gusts, grunted and tossed his head. A new blue horn had replaced the severed black one – the Good Beast was whole again!

A thrill passed over Tom's skin as he kneeled on the ground and gently prised one of the roots from the earth. He placed it carefully in the satchel Daltec had given him. "One ingredient down, three to go," he muttered.

As he stood, he realised he was alone. Raffkor had vanished. Tom fought down a feeling of panic. Touching the ruby in his belt, he felt nothing of Raffkor's presence. Had the huge Beast somehow been blown over the edge? Was that possible?

"Do not worry," said a voice.

Tom spun around and saw Daltec walking towards him. Despite the gusts, his robes didn't move at all.

He's not really here, Tom reminded himself. *He's just a vision.*

A scattering of stones made them both turn around. Tom saw a hand reach over the lip of the mountain top, following by Elenna's dusty face. She brushed herself down as she stood up.

"Quite a climb!" she said. "I didn't want you to have all the fun…" She stopped as she saw the Wizard. "Oh, hello, Daltec! Where's Raffkor?"

"Raffkor is safe," said Daltec. "Now you've freed him from the curse, he has come of age. He will be sent to a distant kingdom where he is needed."

"And how is Vedra?" Tom asked.

Daltec face was grim. "The sickness is spreading all the time," he said. Then he nodded to Tom's satchel. "But you have done well to get this far."

"I won't give up," said Tom, "but first I need to find my shield."

"I can help with that," said Daltec. The young Wizard clicked his fingers, and Tom's shield appeared, floating in the air just in front of him. Tom took it, grateful for the familiar weight on his arm. The surface had a few new scratches, but the tokens were all intact.

"What will happen to all the homeless people?" asked Elenna. "Raffkor destroyed whole villages."

Daltec smiled. "King Hugo is already sending soldiers to help rebuild," he said. "They should be here in a day or two."

"And we need to find Kensa!" said Tom. "She managed to escape."

Daltec shook his head. "Her day of reckoning will come. Your next Quest lies in the Ruby Desert – that's where you'll find the Elixir's next ingredient. Those boiling sands will test your endurance and your courage."

"I'm ready," said Tom.

"Kensa will no doubt have sent another corrupted Beast," said Daltec.

"That witch can poison as many Good Beasts as she likes," said Tom. "While there's blood in my veins, she will not prevail."

Daltec smiled uneasily. "A new Quest awaits you both."

"We're up to it," Elenna said, grinning. Tom would never stop being glad to have her by his side.

With the Wizard's form hovering nearby, and the Starleaf safely stowed, Tom felt a new sense of hope as he descended the Murmuring Peak with Elenna. The task ahead

was daunting – almost impossible –
but he promised himself he would
keep going until the Beast Quest was
complete.

Or until it claimed his life.

Join Tom on the next stage
of the Beast Quest, when he faces

VISLAK
THE SLITHERING
SERPENT!

FREE COLLECTOR CARDS INSIDE!

THE CURSED DRAGON

Series 14: THE CURSED DRAGON
COLLECT THEM ALL!

Tom must face four terrifying Beasts as he
searches for the ingredients for a potion to
rescue the Cursed Dragon.

RAFFKOR
THE STAMPEDING BRUTE

978 1 40832 920 7

VISLAK
THE SLITHERING SERPENT

978 1 40832 921 4

TIKRON
THE JUNGLE MASTER

978 1 40832 922 1

FALRA
THE SNOW PHOENIX

978 1 40832 923 8

SPECIAL BUMPER EDITION:
OKAWA THE RIVER BEAST
Coming in May 2014!

**Watch out for another new
Special Bumper
Edition in
OCTOBER 2014!**

Win an exclusive
Beast Quest T-shirt and goody bag!

In every Beast Quest book the Beast Quest logo is
hidden in one of the pictures. Find the logos in books
79 to 82 and make a note of which pages they appear
on. Write the four page numbers on a postcard and
send it in to us.
Each month we will draw one winner to receive
a Beast Quest T-shirt and goody bag.

THE BEAST QUEST COMPETITION:
The Cursed Dragon
Orchard Books
338 Euston Road, London NW1 3BH
Australian readers should email:
childrens.books@hachette.com.au

New Zealand readers should write to:
Beast Quest Competition
4 Whetu Place, Mairangi Bay, Auckland, NZ
or email: childrensbooks@hachette.co.nz

Only one entry per child.
Final draw: 30 March 2014

You can also enter this competition
via the Beast Quest website: www.beastquest.co.uk

Join the Quest,
Join the Tribe

www.beastquest.co.uk

Have you checked out the Beast Quest website?
It's the place to go for games, downloads, activities,
sneak previews and lots of fun!

You can read all about your favourite Beasts,
download free screensavers and desktop wallpapers
for your computer, and even challenge your friends
to a Beast Tournament.

Sign up to the newsletter at www.beastquest.co.uk
to receive exclusive extra content and the
opportunity to enter special members-only
competitions. We'll send you up-to-date info on all
the Beast Quest books, including the next exciting
series which features four brand-new Beasts!